Underwater Mayhem

MASK are assigned to protect The President of the Peaceful Nations Alliance but peace is the last thing on Miles Mayhem's mind.

© 1986 Kenner Parker Toys Inc. (KPT). All rights reserved.
Published in Great Britain by World International Publishing Limited.
An Egmont Company, Egmont House, P.O. Box 111,
Great Ducie Street, Manchester M60 3BL.
Printed in Italy. SBN 7235 8816 3.
1st reprint 1987.

MASK™

UNDERWATER MAYHEM

MASK had just been given a very important mission.
The President of the Peaceful Nations Alliance was
to visit a special underwater complex and they had to
guard him, which meant that they must energise their
masks.

The first part of their mission was to escort the President to the complex. To anyone who didn't know how good MASK was at its job, the President looked unprotected. The MASK vehicles Rhino and Gator were, however, perhaps the best guard in the world!

The trio of vehicles arrived safely at the top secret docking area and transferred into the Aqua-bubble for the last leg of the trip to the complex. So far, so good, Matt thought to himself as the bubble slowly sank towards its target.

Suddenly, from out of the cover of giant underwater reeds, moved the Piranha! "Mayhem's underwater attack vehicle!" Sato exclaimed as the first blast from the VENOM machine hit the Aqua-bubble.

Caught off-guard by the Piranha attack, MASK didn't notice that Cliff Dagger, VENOM's hot-shot agent, had swum underneath the Aqua-bubble. "Torch on!" he said as a jet of flame arced out of his mask.

Trapped inside the bubble, MASK faced a double-sided attack. The Piranha continued to fire on the engine while Dagger used his Torch Mask to heat the underside of the bubble! My flame is so hot that it even works under water, Dagger thought with a smirk.

"Luckily, they began their attack too late," Matt observed as the Aqua-bubble glided into the massive airlock in the complex.

"The big problem is," said a worried Sato, "that this was supposed to be a top secret visit. There is no one else at the complex."

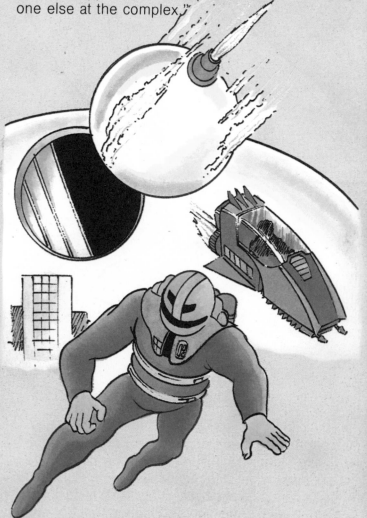

"Ever since the PNA built this complex we have kept sensors here. When they reported yesterday that everyone was being sent away, we knew something big was being planned. But to capture MASK and the President . . . that is a super-bonus!" sneered VENOM's leader.

Inside the complex, MASK tried to make the most of a bad situation. "Our first job is to protect the President," Matt said, "even if it means the end of MASK."

"Earthquake!" yelled Hayes as the whole complex was shaken by a powerful shock wave. "And I bet I can guess the real cause of it."

"It looks like VENOM are throwing everything they have at us," Matt complained, "and we're trapped here – helpless."

"Now we're in for it," said Hayes, pointing to a crack that was inching its way along the protective dome.

"We've only moments to seal it," Matt yelled.

"The foodstore!" Sato shouted, and ran into a large building facing them.

"What the . . ?" Hayes began to say but Matt interrupted him.

"It's okay, Dusty, Sato always does that when he gets an idea."

"Well, I sure hope it's a good one. That wall won't last much longer."

"I think I know what he's doing," Matt said as he watched Sato use his Lifter Mask to snap one of the pipes carrying the icy cold air into the food plant. "That gas is about 10 degrees below freezing point."

"Got it!" Hayes yelled as he watched the freezing gas turn the water near the crack into solid ice. The MASK agents watched as the gas quickly formed an icy seal on the crack and saved the complex.

"If we could cripple VENOM's weapons they wouldn't stand a chance against us," Hayes said as he made for the air-lock. Moments later he was swimming towards the Piranha. Time to give VENOM a 'shock', he joked to himself as he fired his Backlash Mask.

Immediately, a shock wave shot out from the mask. As it hit the Piranha, the VENOM machine began to shake. "Better back off," said Rax as he moved his machine away.

"Strike one for MASK," Hayes murmured with a smile.

"I have lost the element of surprise," Mayhem complained. "I had hoped to capture the President and take over the complex but now I know I have only one chance . . ." As Mayhem said this he pressed a button and fired a Mega-bomb at the complex!

"Anything the Mega-bomb touches it absorbs and destroys," Mayhem said with a smirk. "Once it touches the outside of the complex the President and MASK will be no more." As Mayhem spoke, the Mega-bomb moved ever closer to the complex.

"Mega-bomb!" shouted Trakker as he spotted the dreadful device moving towards them. "Dusty, Sato . . . we have one chance . . ."

Sato interrupted him. "We're way ahead of you, Matt," he said, and the two MASK agents began using their masks to free the ice around the complex.

Soon, a large chunk of ice snapped off and began to float upwards. "Ice is lighter than water, that's why you always have ice on top," Sato said as the icy chunk drifted into the path of the Mega-bomb.

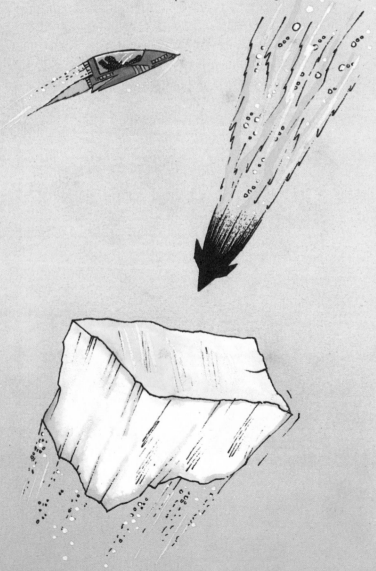

As planned, the ice drifted into the Mega-bomb, causing it to explode harmlessly outside the complex. "Mayhem's used up all his underwater weapons so he won't bother us again, just yet," Trakker observed.

With VENOM gone, Hayes re-entered the complex
and joined his friends and the President. "Well done,
MASK," said the President.

"Thank you, Sir," replied Trakker, "but we were
only doing our duty."

"And speaking of duty," continued the President, "I still have an inspection tour to make. We can't let a little thing like an attack by VENOM stop us!"

As the group made the inspection they were all happy to know that VENOM had once again been outwitted!